WAS THAT CHRISTMAS?
Written by Hilary McKay
Illustrated by Amanda Harvey

British Library Cataloguing in Publication Data
A catalogue record of this book is available from the British Library.

ISBN 0340 86626 8

Text copyright © Hilary McKay 2001
Illustrations copyright © Amanda Harvey 2001

The right of Hilary McKay to be identified as the author
and Amanda Harvey as the illustrator of this Work
has been asserted by them in accordance with
the Copyright, Designs and Patents Act 1988.

First edition published 2001
This mini hardback edition published 2002
10 9 8 7 6 5 4 3 2 1

Published by Hodder Children's Books,
a division of Hodder Headline Limited,
338 Euston Road, London NW1 3BH

Printed in Hong Kong

WAS THAT CHRISTMAS?

Written by **Hilary McKay**

Illustrated by **Amanda Harvey**

*Hodder
Children's
Books*

A division of Hodder Headline Limited

Once upon a time, there was a baby called Bella and a kitten called Black Jack. Bella and Black Jack were too small to know about Christmas.

Then Bella and Black Jack were both one-year-old.
They chewed up the wrapping paper and made lots of noise.
They still did not know about Christmas.

Next they were two, big enough to run and climb.
They climbed up the Christmas tree and it fell down flat.
They still did not know about Christmas.

When they were three, Bella started play school.
At play school Bella found out all about Christmas.

Bella told Black Jack, 'Christmas is when it snows and Santa Claus comes on a sleigh pulled by reindeer. He has a huge brown sack full of presents for children!'

Black Jack hunched up his shoulders the way he did when he was cross. 'Will Santa Claus bring presents for Black Jack too?' asked Bella.

'Of course,' said Bella's mum.

At last it was really nearly Christmas.

At play school they did a Christmas play with shepherds and angels and Little Baby Jesus in a bed of real hay. Bella was a shepherd and Black Jack was her lamb. Everyone clapped and clapped.

'What is next?' asked all the children.
'Santa Claus!' guessed Bella and, sure enough, the door opened
and someone stepped in.

SANTA CLAUS HAD COME
TO PLAY SCHOOL!

Santa Claus looked just like Santa
Claus should.
He had a long white beard and
a huge brown sack.
'Where are the reindeer?'
asked Bella.

Santa Claus said he hadn't
brought his reindeer because there
wasn't any snow.
'No snow?' said Bella. 'No reindeer?'
'No,' said Santa Claus.

The children looked at each other and then Bella (who was the bravest) asked, 'What is in your sack?'

Santa Claus opened his sack and gave presents to all the children.

Santa Claus had not brought a
present for Black Jack.

On the way home, Bella suddenly started to cry. She roared.
She roared and her tears got all mixed up with the rain.
'Whatever is the matter?' said Bella's mum.

'Santa Claus didn't bring a present for Black Jack,' roared Bella,
'and he didn't bring his reindeer and there isn't any snow!'
'Oh, Bella!'
'Has Santa Claus really been?' roared Bella. 'Was that Christmas?'

Suddenly, Bella's mother understood and she knelt
down in the rainy street and hugged Bella and said,
'That wasn't Christmas! That was just the
beginning of Christmas!'

'What we have to do now is . . .

. . . post the cards through all
our friends' letter boxes . . .

. . . bake mince pies,

ice the cake,

hang up the streamers

and fetch the tree!'

'And now is it Christmas?' asked Bella, when she and Black Jack were lying by the fire at the end of the day.

'No, no!' said Gran, who had come to visit. 'Christmas is just getting started! Tomorrow we have got to . . .

. . . go into town,
choose the crackers,

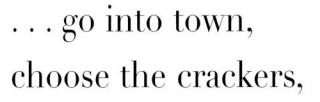

buy presents for your mother and father,

sing with the band,

shout Happy Christmas to
everyone we meet,

and ride home on the bus
when it's nearly dark and
all the lights are shining.'

'Now it must be Christmas!' said Bella, when she and Gran were home at last and the presents were hidden safely under her bed. 'And what about Santa Claus?'

'What about Santa Claus?' asked Bella's father.

'He came to play school and didn't bring Black Jack a present!' said Bella.

'Are you sure?' asked Bella's father. 'Because it's not Christmas yet! You and I have still got to . . .

. . . hang up the Christmas nuts
for the birds,

fix the tree lights,

eat sausage rolls hot out
of the oven,

mend the camp bed that Gran always
sleeps on and says she enjoys,

and make a snowman!'
'With what?' asked Bella.
'Look outside,' said her father.

It took all the next day to finish these things and Bella was
so tired at the end of them that she and Black Jack nearly
fell asleep on the floor.

'Now,' said her father, 'we have to tell you about
Santa Claus!'

'Santa Claus,' said her gran, 'comes when it snows . . .'
'It's snowing!' cried Bella.
'. . . on a sleigh pulled by reindeer . . .'
'I knew he did!'
'He has a huge brown sack full of
presents for cats . . .' Bella
hugged Black Jack.

'. . . and children, of course.'
'But when?' asked Bella.

'Tonight!' said her mother.

'Is it Christmas then?' asked Bella.
'Is it Christmas
      at last?'

'Oh no!' said her mother and father and gran all together.
'First you must leave Santa Claus a mince pie and a
sausage roll,

a glass of wine,

a teabag for a cup of tea,

and a carrot chopped in slices for the reindeer.

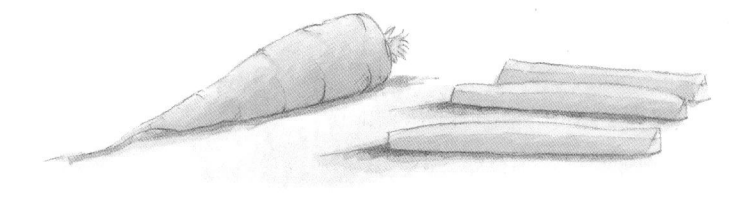

Then you kiss
    us goodnight,

and climb the stairs,

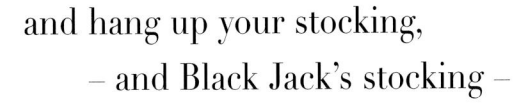

and hang up your stocking,
    – and Black Jack's stocking –

close your
    eyes and
    go to sleep
        until morning.

And then . . .

That's Christmas!'